ZIBBY PAYNE

& THE TRIO TROUBLE

Published by Lobster Press™
1620 Sherbrooke Street West, Suites C & D
Montréal, Québec   H3H 1C9
Tel. (514) 904-1100 • Fax (514) 904-1101 • www.lobsterpress.com

Publisher: Alison Fripp
Editors: Alison Fripp & Meghan Nolan
Editorial Assistants: Lindsay Cornish, Shiran Teitelbaum & Emma Stephen
Graphic Design & Production: Tammy Desnoyers

Library and Archives Canada Cataloguing in Publication

Bell, Alison
     Zibby Payne & the trio trouble / Alison Bell.

(Zibby Payne series)
ISBN 978-1-897073-78-0

     I. Title. II. Title: Zibby Payne and the trio trouble. III.
Series: Bell, Alison. Zibby Payne series.

PZ7.B41528Zit 2008   j813'.6   C2007-904765-3

To my father, W.D. Bell.

– Alison Bell

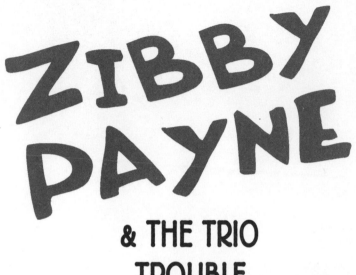

ZIBBY PAYNE

& THE TRIO
TROUBLE

written by

Alison Bell

Lobster Press ™

CHAPTER 1

A RUSH TO SCHOOL

It was only 7:20 a.m. on a Monday morning, and somebody was at Zibby Payne's front door. And that someone was desperate to get in.

First came the ring of the doorbell.

Then a rap on the door.

Then an urgent pounding.

"Who is it?" Zibby asked herself in the middle of pouring a bowl of Cheerios. She ran to the front door, flung it open, and found her best friend Sarah.

"Sarah!" she yelled happily, giving her a hug. " Give me twenty!"

The two girls performed their own personal secret greeting of a series of high fives, low fives, a clap, and a spin. When they were done, Zibby asked, "So how come you're here?"

"My mom got a call from Miss Cannon this morning asking me if I could show a new girl around school before class started," Sarah replied, following Zibby back into the kitchen. "So of course, that means you, too! I came over and was hoping we could walk to school together. But we've got to hurry – I'm supposed to meet her on the blacktop at 7:30."

"Whoa – that's in 10 minutes," said Zibby, checking the

kitchen clock. She looked longingly at the Cheerios she wouldn't have time to eat now, then grabbed her backpack and slung it over her shoulder.

"Okay, I'm ready," said Zibby, glad that she wasn't one of those girls who sat around primping for hours and happy that she could be ready to leave in a moment's notice.

"Wait – our shoes," said Sarah. "Quick!"

"Oh yeah," nodded Zibby.

Zibby kicked off one of her Converse low-tops while Sarah slipped off one of her zebra-striped ballet flats, and the two girls put on one of the other's shoes. Shoe swapping was a tradition they'd shared since second grade. And luckily, their feet had grown at the same rate since then and they both wore size six.

"And what about your cleats?" asked Sarah.

Zibby, a tomboy, often played soccer at recess and lunch with the boys. And since she couldn't play soccer in mismatched shoes, she brought her Adidas cleats to school every day so that she could change into them – when she didn't forget to pack them, that is.

"Got them right here," Zibby said as she patted her backpack. "But thanks for the reminder."

The two girls headed back out to the entry hall. But before they reached the front door, Zibby stopped at the stairs leading to the second story. "Bye everyone! Got to go to school early today!" she yelled up to her mom, dad, and two brothers as she zipped out the door with Sarah.

Zibby's stomach growled and she felt a flash of annoyance at having to leave in such a rush and without her breakfast. But then, she remembered something. A promise she'd made to herself after she recently threw a big party that was supposedly for "everyone," and yet she'd managed to leave a couple of girls out and hurt their feelings. A promise to be a "Better, Kinder Zibby" for the rest of her sixth-grade year. And now was a perfect time to be this new, improved person.

Besides, it was exciting to have a new student in their class. It got boring being around the same kids all the time, especially since Zibby had known most in her grade since kindergarten.

"So, I wonder what the new girl is like – do you know anything about her?" asked Zibby as they hustled down the street to Lincoln Elementary, which was only a few blocks away.

"I don't even know her name," said Sarah. "Miss Cannon didn't tell my mom anything."

"No matter what she's like, I'm going to be really nice to her because it must be hard to start a new school – espccially in the middle of the year," Zibby said.

"I'd hate it," said Sarah. "Can you imagine how scary it would be?"

Zibby shook her head. "We're lucky we've never had to move." Both girls had lived in the same place their entire lives, and the only time they had to worry about meeting new people was at summer camp.

Zibby began to speed up as the girls got closer to the school. "Let's make sure we get there on time so she's not just standing all alone," she said. "And who knows? Maybe she'll be our next best friend. I mean, we won't swap shoes with her or teach her our secret greeting, of course, but we can invite her to our sleepovers and we can go roller-skating with her. Maybe she even likes soccer."

"Don't get too carried away," interrupted Sarah. She knew Zibby had a tendency to go overboard with her Very Good Ideas and Grand Plans. "We haven't even met her!"

"Well, hopefully we'll at least *like* her," said Zibby, toning it down good-naturedly.

The girls ran onto the school blacktop where the students met every day and lined up for class, but the blacktop was bare. There was no sign of a new girl, or any girl for that matter.

"Where is she?" asked Zibby, looking around.

"I don't know," said Sarah. "Miss Cannon said she'd be here."

The two girls waited, with Zibby impatiently tapping her foot, when slowly but surely the blacktop filled up with students, parents, and teachers – but still, there was no new girl.

"That stinks," said Sarah. "And we got here early and everything."

"Yeah," said Zibby, sighing and still searching the blacktop, her curiosity running away with her. What would this new girl look like? Sound like? What did she like to do? And most of all, would she be good friend material?

Shoot, she thought to herself. Here she was, so ready and willing to be kind and helpful to the new girl – even on an empty stomach – and she wasn't getting the chance! She'd have to wait – and she hated waiting – a little bit longer to meet this mystery girl.

CHAPTER 2

A DRAMATIC ENTRANCE

"What happened to the new girl?" Sarah and Zibby asked Miss Cannon as soon as their teacher appeared on the blacktop.

"I'm sorry, girls – her mom called to say they had to fill out some papers at the district office and they'd be a little late," replied Miss Cannon. "You can show her around at recess instead, if that's okay."

"Sure," said Zibby, forgetting about her hunger and just glad there really *was* going to be a new girl.

Zibby and Sarah followed Miss Cannon into class and took their seats. Zibby sat in the front of the class; Sarah sat in the back by the door. Every year Sarah specifically asked for a seat near the door so she could scoot out of the classroom fast and be one of the first in line at the cafeteria, which was always jammed. And since all the teachers liked Sarah, they always accommodated her wish. Zibby packed a lunch every day, so she didn't have to worry about the cafeteria rush. She was addicted to salmon and cucumber sandwiches, or on days when she wanted some variety, salmon and *pickle* sandwiches.

Zibby kept turning in her seat, swiveling her head and looking for the new girl to come through the door when Miss

Cannon walked in front of the class and cleared her throat. Zibby now focused her attention on her teacher.

"Good morning, class," Miss Cannon said. "I have some exciting news. We have a new student joining us. Her name is Gertrude Long, and she's going to be sitting right here." Miss Cannon pointed to the empty desk in the front with a stack of textbooks on it.

Gertrude? Cool name, Zibby thought to herself even though the other kids snickered and whispered, "Gertrude?" Zibby was partial to old-lady names because her real name was Elizabeth after her grandmother on her mom's side, and her middle name was Mildred, courtesy of some great-aunt of her dad's. When you put those two names together, Elizabeth Mildred, you couldn't get any more old-lady sounding than that.

"She should be here any moment," continued Miss Cannon. "And I know when she arrives, you're all going to give her a warm welcome."

All the kids started chattering among themselves about the newest addition to their class when just then, a tall, thin girl rushed into the room.

Zibby did a double take. This girl didn't look like an "old lady" Gertrude-type at all. She had long dark brown hair, parted in the middle, big blue eyes, and she was wearing an animal-print sweater, fitted knee-length skirt, tights, and big clunky combat boots.

"I love her look," Zibby said to herself in approval. Most sixth grade girls wore mini-skirts and short tops – a trend that had started this year and that Zibby stayed away from since she pretty much only wore jeans and T-shirts. It was a relief to see someone else dressing differently – another score for the new girl!

"Welcome, Gertrude. I'm glad you made it," smiled Miss Cannon. "And now, if you'll take your seat," she motioned to the empty desk, "we can get started on our math."

Gertrude looked at the desk, then up at the ceiling, and then frowned.

"I'm sorry, but I can't sit there," said Gertrude firmly.

"Why not?" asked Miss Cannon, raising her eyebrows in surprise.

"Because of *that*," said Gertrude, pointing to a vent that was located on the ceiling directly above the desk. "The air coming from it carries dust particles that aggravate my sinuses – my doctor said I can't sit by any vents."

"Oh," said Miss Cannon, pulling on her pinky finger, which she did whenever she got nervous. "Well, if it's a health concern, then I guess you'll have to switch with someone," Miss Cannon said.

"Rad, thanks," said Gertrude. "Actually, I need the seat farthest away from the vent," she continued, "which would be ... " she surveyed the room " ... that one!" She pointed her finger to the back left-hand side of the room, right at Sarah's desk!

Sarah blinked and looked at Miss Cannon, who paused for a second and then nodded.

"Hey wait a minute ... " Sarah stood up, protesting.

"This is *my* seat. I always sit in this spot."

"I'm sorry, Sarah, but I think we're going to have to help Gertrude out on this one," said Miss Cannon, pulling on her pinky again.

Sarah set her mouth in a line, then bent down and quickly cleaned out her desk with jerky motions, piling her books, notebooks, and flowered pencil cases on the desk. She gathered everything up in her arms, stomped across the room, and dumped her things with a slam onto her new desk.

Gertrude, who had been waiting in the front of the class, hesitated for a moment. Then she shot Sarah an apologetic glance and walked over to sit down at Sarah's old desk.

Zibby watched as Sarah glared at Gertrude and began stuffing her belongings into the new desk.

Uh oh, thought Zibby. *Gertrude's definitely making an impression on Sarah – a really bad one!*

CHAPTER 3

DRAWING ON DEMAND

"Can you believe her?" Sarah hurried over to Zibby as soon as the recess bell rang. "After we ran to school early to show her around, she steals my seat. Now I'm going to get dust particles on *me*. And I'm going to be late for lunch every day!"

Zibby could see Sarah's points, and she would have been bugged if she had to give up her seat too, just because it was a hassle. On the other hand, if Gertrude would get sick sitting near a vent, then it really wasn't her fault she couldn't sit there.

"I know," Zibby said sympathetically. "But at least you don't have a sinus problem, so the vent won't bother you. And I'll bet if you walk a little faster when the bell rings, you'll still beat the line."

"I guess so," said Sarah, sighing.

"Hey, if you want, I'll run to the cafeteria every day and save a place in line for you," offered Zibby. Due to all her soccer playing, she was faster than Sarah, plus she had the fancy footwork to maneuver around the kids as they shuffled down the hallway.

"Thanks, Zibby, that's nice of you to offer, but I'll be okay," replied Sarah. "I'm probably making too much of it anyway – I'll get over it."

"That's good," Zibby exclaimed, "because we're still supposed to show Gertrude around this recess and it will be easier if you aren't mad at her." She looked around the room, which had already emptied because everyone had gone out to recess. "If we can find her, that is."

The girls walked outside and found Gertrude standing by the wall talking to Amber and Camille. Amber and Camille used to be good friends of Zibby and Sarah's, but lately they had changed, and not for the better, in Zibby's opinion. They were way too much into short skirts, lip gloss, and boys for Zibby's taste. Plus, she never knew what potentially snotty thing was going to pop out of their mouths.

Zibby and Sarah joined the girls just as Amber was asking Gertrude, "So do you have really bad health problems?"

"Oh, no," Gertrude replied. "I'm just sensitive to recycled air, that's all."

When Gertrude saw Zibby and Sarah join the group, she gave them a big smile. "Thanks for giving up your desk," Gertrude said to Sarah. "I didn't know it would be such a big thing – are you sure you're okay with it?"

"It's fine," said Sarah, looking happier now that Gertrude had apologized. "We should introduce ourselves officially – I'm Sarah and this is Zibby."

"Hey, there," smiled Zibby.

"If you don't mind," said Amber, edging closer to Gertrude, "we were just asking Gertrude a little bit about herself. So where'd you get your outfit?" she asked. "It's very ... um ... unique."

As soon as Zibby heard the word "unique," she began to get a bad feeling. That was Amber's code word for ugly.

"At this really rad vintage store back home," said Gertrude. "Everyone at my school shopped there."

"Vintage – you mean they're *used*?" asked Camille, wrinkling her nose.

"Someone *else* wore them before you?" asked Amber, backing away.

For an instant, Zibby wondered if she should step in to protect Gertrude from the two Queens of Mean, but then Gertrude smoothly replied, "Not *used* – I think of them as *pre-loved*. All the stars are wearing pre-loved clothing. It's totally in right now."

"*Pre-loved*, huh?" asked Amber, now looking interested. "I'll have to check these clothes out."

"You should – you'd look good in them," said Gertrude.

Normally Zibby would find any conversation about fashion boring, but she was fascinated by how Gertrude wasn't letting Amber or Camille get to her. *Go Gertrude*, Zibby thought to herself.

"So where are you from?" Zibby asked her.

"A town up north called Oakville."

"Sounds small ... and boring," sniffed Amber.

"It sounds *pretty* to me," said Zibby, giving Amber the evil eye.

"It is." Gertrude smiled at Zibby. "It's got a lake, and the town is filled with lots of historic buildings, cool book shops, and health food stores."

"Health food stores?" asked Amber. "I luv those. That's where all the celebs shop. So are you into health food?"

"Oh ... well ... sure," said Gertrude. "Everyone ate that way back home."

"It must have been hard to move," said Sarah.

"Yeah, but my dad got a new job down here so we had to," she said.

"What does he do?" asked Amber.

"He's a painter," answered Gertrude.

"*A house* painter?" Amber frowned. "*My* dad's an attorney."

"Um, no, he's a *painter* – like an artist painter. I'm an artist too – I draw and paint," said Gertrude.

"Wow," said Zibby and Sarah at the same time. Zibby didn't enjoy art – she could hardly draw a stick person – but she admired anyone who was creative. And Sarah was a total Crafts Person who always had some sort of art project going.

Amber, however, didn't look impressed. She pulled out her signature lip gloss – Groovy Grapilicious – and applied some to her lips in a bored way.

"In fact, I just won a big award for one of my paintings," said Gertrude. "I beat out hundreds of other kids, some as old as eighteen."

"That's awesome," said Zibby.

Even Amber raised her eyebrows as if she now might be the teeniest bit impressed. Then she said, "Hey, if you're really an artist, show us."

"Yeah, be artistic," commanded Camille.

That's not fair, thought Zibby, *putting Gertrude on the spot her very first day at school, especially after bugging her about her clothes.*

"Hey, Gertrude is not some contestant on a reality TV show," Zibby was about to protest when she was cut off by Gertrude, who said, "Sure, why not? Does anyone have any paper and something I can use for support, like a book or magazine?"

"Just a sec," said Amber, and she ran into the classroom. She came back with a piece of notebook paper and a magazine. "Here," she handed them over to Gertrude, "but just be careful because this is my brand-new collector's issue of *Teen Scene* magazine with BB5 on the cover. Isn't Fabrio a mega-cutie?"

Typical, thought Zibby. Amber *would* care about protecting a trashy gossip magazine, especially one featuring the BB5 – a pop boy band that Zibby couldn't stand – and its lead singer Fabrio Fabricio.

"I'll be careful," promised Gertrude. She whipped out a marker from a small purse strung across her shoulder, put the paper on top of the magazine, did a quick sketch, then signed it "GL."

"There you go – your portrait," said Gertrude as she handed everything back to Amber.

Amber studied the drawing and then sniffed. "Not bad. But my nose isn't quite that big. Actually it's just like JLo's.

And *TV Tonight* recently voted her as having the best celebrity nose."

"It really does look like you," said Sarah, ignoring Amber's comment. She and Zibby were studying the portrait some more when Amber let out a huge shriek.

CHAPTER 4

A SURPRISE AT SARAH'S HOUSE

"You totally destroyed Fabrio's gorgeousness!" Amber wailed to Gertrude, thrusting the magazine at her. "Your marker bled through the paper and put black dots all over his face. Now he looks like he has the chicken pox!"

"Oh no – I didn't mean to mess up your magazine," apologized Gertrude.

"It's not a *magazine*," yelled Amber. "It's a *collector's issue* my dad got me because one of his clients knows BB5. Come on," she turned to Camille and yanked her arm. "Let's go. I've got to call my dad and see if he can get me another copy."

As soon as Amber and Camille were out of ear shot, Zibby snorted with laughter. "I'm not trying to be a jerk, but that was so funny. If you only knew how much she loves that band."

"I think I got the idea pretty well," said Gertrude dryly.

"And," Zibby continued, "she totally deserved it for forcing you to draw on the spot like that!"

"She's always bossing everyone around," said Sarah.

"I *am* sorry about it though," said Gertrude.

"Don't even worry," said Zibby. "Her dad probably has

about a dozen other copies lying around he can give her."

"I've never even heard of Fabrio or BB5," said Gertrude. "At home, my friends and I only listened to indie or classic rock."

"I love classic rock too," said Zibby. "Especially the Beatles and the Eagles."

"The Beatles are totally rad – they're one of my favorite bands," said Gertrude.

"Hey, I'm going over to Sarah's today after school, and you should come too. I've got a lot of their CDs on my iPod, and we can listen to them over there," said Zibby, excited about getting to know Gertrude better and wanting to make her feel welcome – especially after Amber's rude outburst. "What do you think, Sarah?"

Sarah hesitated, then said, "Sure, come on over."

"You're okay about the desk?" Gertrude asked. "I could give it back."

"Oh no, your sinuses need it. Forget about it," said Sarah, a little too quickly.

Gertrude called her mom on her cell phone to ask if she could go over to Sarah's, and her mom said yes, so it was all set.

* * *

That afternoon, Sarah's mom was waiting for them in the pick-up lane in her white mini-van.

"Wow, that's a big car – my mom drives a Prius. Most

everyone does back home," said Gertrude as soon as she saw what Sarah's mom was driving.

"Is that one of those hybrid cars?" asked Zibby. She'd been seeing some around town and thought they were a good idea even though her mom drove a mini-van too.

"Yeah – they're good for the environment and cost less to fill up," said Gertrude.

"My mom needs a mini-van," said Sarah, "because she's always taking me, my sister, and our friends around. We wouldn't all fit in a smaller car."

"You could always walk more," said Gertrude. "I used to walk everywhere back home."

"We usually do walk home from school," said Sarah, a bit too sharply, Zibby thought. "Today it's special that we're getting picked up because my mom had to drop by the school anyway to get something from the office."

Sarah's mom opened the sliding car door for the girls, and they piled into the van.

Sarah introduced Gertrude to her mom as the girls buckled up.

"Nice to meet you – and I love your name," said Mrs. Schroeder. "Is it a family name?"

"Um, oh – no," said Gertrude. "I was named after Gertrude Stein – a famous feminist writer."

"'A rose is a rose is a rose,'" said Mrs. Schroeder. "That was one of her famous lines – it's almost all I know about her."

"She was a genius – and a patron of the arts," said Gertrude. "She hung out with all the leading artists of the time, like Picasso."

Cool, thought Zibby. She didn't know much about Picasso – only that he was the artist who put eyes where ears should be – but she was envious of Gertrude. Not that she minded being named after her grandmother, whom she loved very much, but it'd sure be a lot more interesting to be named after someone famous.

For the rest of the drive, Zibby and Sarah pointed out some local landmarks to Gertrude, like the park and the library, and then they talked about a special landmark in Sarah's very own home.

"Wait until you see it – you're going to love it," said Zibby. "Everyone does!"

"What is it?" asked Gertrude.

"You'll have to wait and see," said Sarah, smiling mysteriously.

They were talking about Sarah's well-stocked snack pantry, which everyone in sixth grade knew was the best in town. At any given time you could find chips, pretzels, granola bars, crackers, cookies, fruit strips, and sometimes even homemade brownies.

When they got to Sarah's house, Sarah rushed into the kitchen and threw open the door to the cupboard.

"Get ready to worship at the altar of the Cabinet of Carbs!" yelled Zibby.

But instead of picking out her favorite food like everyone else, Gertrude just stood there, staring. And then, she did The Unthinkable.

CHAPTER 5

FOOD FOR THOUGHT

Gertrude shook her head and backed away from the cabinet.

"No thanks. I can't eat any of this," she reported matter-of-factly.

"Really?" Sarah's face fell. "Why?"

"Like I told Amber, I eat health food, not junk food."

"It's not *all* junk food," protested Sarah. "Granola bars and pretzels are okay to eat, especially if you balance them out with fruits and vegetables during the day. My mom always says, 'everything in moderation.'"

"I guess that's true, but still … I think I'll pass," said Gertrude.

"Oh." Sarah looked a little annoyed – as well as disappointed – that anyone could reject the Cabinet of Carbs.

Zibby herself wasn't disappointed, but she was surprised anyone would turn down Mrs. Schroeder's famous snack shelf. But then, she figured, Gertrude was *so* unique, what with being an artist and wearing "pre-loved" clothes and being named after a famous writer – of course she didn't eat the normal kind of food everyone else at Lincoln Elementary did.

"What kind of snacks do you eat then?" Zibby asked.

"Oh um ... you know, dried fruit, veggies, fruit, um ... and veggie ... chips," Gertrude answered.

"Veggie chips? I've never had those," said Zibby. "Are they good?"

"Um, oh yeah, they're rad," said Gertrude quickly.

"I'll have to try them," said Zibby, wondering how they'd taste dunked in her favorite sour cream and onion dip with crunched-up Fritos on top.

Meanwhile Sarah was fishing out apples from the refrigerator. "Would you like one of these?"

"Is it organic?" asked Gertrude. "Those pesticides they use can be so nasty to your body."

"No," said Sarah. "All we have are the normal pesticide kind." She handed one to Gertrude.

"Oh, well, thanks," said Gertrude. "I'll just give it a quick wash then to make sure it's safe." She walked over to the sink and ran water over the apple.

Sarah grabbed a bag of pretzels and some cookies from the cabinet and handed a cookie to Zibby. Zibby felt awkward eating junk food in front of Gertrude, but on the other hand, double-stuffed Oreos were just too good to resist.

After the girls had eaten, they went upstairs to Sarah's room to listen to the Beatles and to talk. Zibby and Gertrude chatted nonstop and learned all sorts of things they had in common. They both had an older brother and a younger brother, they both loved to read – *Harriet the Spy* was their all-time favorite book – their mothers were both freelance writers, and Gertrude had even once been a tomboy.

"Did you play soccer?" asked Zibby after filling Gertrude in on her love of the game.

"No, but in second grade, all I wanted to do was climb trees and play hand ball," she said. "I even cut my own hair off because my mom wouldn't let me get a super short haircut," she said.

"No way! Me, too," said Zibby. "A couple of months ago I hacked off a part of my hair right here," she motioned to the spot above her left ear, "and it looked horrible! I had to wear a hat for weeks until it grew in, so that I didn't look like a total freak."

"In pictures of me from back then, you can't even tell I was a girl," said Gertrude.

"Some kids like Amber bug me about being a tomboy," said Zibby. "But I don't care what they think."

"Who wants to be like everyone else anyway? Not me!" said Gertrude.

"Me neither!" sang out Zibby.

Zibby could have happily gone on talking to Gertrude for hours, but at 4:00, Gertrude's mom called and said she had to go home to help unpack boxes.

"Isn't she amazing?" Zibby asked Sarah once Gertrude had gone.

"Hardly!" said Sarah, wrinkling up her face. "I don't like her. I mean, I was ready to forgive her for taking my desk, but then she criticized my mom's car and pretty much said how bad our food is. I think she's rude!"

"Oh," said, Zibby, taken aback. "Well, she is picky about

what she eats. But I don't know if she's rude. I think she just has strong opinions."

"And all she does is go on and on about how much better everything was where she used to live," continued Sarah. "It's so annoying. Maybe she should just go back there."

"Whoa – maybe she's homesick and that's why she talks about Oakville so much," said Zibby.

"*And* she pretty much ignored me all afternoon," Sarah continued as if she hadn't heard what Zibby said. "All she did was talk to you – and she was at *my* house!"

"No way, Sarah, that's not true," Zibby started to say, but then she stopped. She'd been chatting away so intently with Gertrude that she only realized just then that Sarah hadn't been a part of their conversation. "You were just being quiet, that's all. I'm sure she would have said a lot to you if you'd been talking as much as I was. You know how much I love to talk – and how loud I can be too!"

"Whatever," said Sarah. "All I can say is, of all the new girls who could have moved here, how come we had to get a dud like her?"

Zibby was quiet. She hated to disagree with Sarah about anything, but she thought Sarah was being too critical. Maybe Gertrude was a little bit irritating about her food habits and how great everything was back home, but Zibby still liked her anyway. In fact, she thought Gertrude was one of the most interesting girls she'd ever met.

CHAPTER 6

THREE'S A CROWD

Zibby felt funny liking Gertrude when Sarah didn't, but she didn't worry about it too much. She figured that the two of them had just gotten off to a bad start, and that the more Sarah got to know Gertrude, the more her feelings would change.

But every time the three of them were together, it seemed like something Not Totally Terrible but Slightly Uncomfortable Enough would happen that would make Sarah dislike Gertrude even more ... and then get annoyed with Zibby, too!

Like when their class went to the library for their weekly book exchange and Zibby sat down on the love seat and Gertrude sat down next to her. Sarah tried to fit in on the other side of Zibby, but there wasn't enough room, and Sarah went off in a huff.

Or when they had to break into pairs in gym class for the "Sit-up Challenge," and Gertrude asked Zibby to be her partner ... right before Sarah did. So Sarah wound up partnering with a weird boy named Harold Klinkstar and looking put out during all forty-six of her sit-ups and all fifty-one of Harold's.

No wonder three is an odd number, thought Zibby to

herself. *Somebody is always the odd girl out when there are three.*

On Friday, however, Zibby had something even bigger to think about. Miss Cannon assigned the class a big English project due in a week – making a journal based on a book they'd just read, *Where The Red Fern Grows*. Zibby wasn't concerned about the journal entries – she loved to write – but Miss Cannon said they also had to illustrate their entries, which *did* worry her.

"I stink at art," she groused to Gertrude as they walked out of school together on Friday afternoon. "I just know the illustrations are going to lower my grade."

"Come on, no one's terrible at art," said Gertrude. "Everyone can be an artist."

"Not me!" yelled Zibby in protest. "My parents forgot to give me the art gene. I think they were a lot more successful giving me the *loud* gene."

"Luckily I like loud people," smiled Gertrude. "And I'm sure you're a better artist than you think. All you need is confidence. And maybe someone to help you. I could give you some pointers if you want."

"That would be great," said Zibby, cheering up. "How about today?" She didn't feel bad asking Gertrude to help since Gertrude didn't have to do the journal because she hadn't read the book yet – one advantage to being the new girl.

Gertrude checked with her mom, who said yes, and the two girls walked over to Zibby's house. But as soon as they got inside, Zibby, trying to be a Good Hostess, felt a stab of panic. "Oh no! What are you going to eat?" she asked Gertrude. "We don't have anything that's organic or fat-free or anything."

"That's okay, I brought some veggie chips with me," said Gertrude. She reached into her backpack and pulled out a bag. "Want to try them?" She held them out to Zibby.

Zibby wrinkled up her nose and hesitantly tasted one, then smiled. "They're good," she said. However, she was in the mood for more than just dried up vegetable slices. She pulled out some mint chip ice cream from the freezer.

"I think I need some ice cream to get my artistic juices flowing. I hope you don't mind if I have some," she said. She dished out a big scoop of ice cream and then topped it off with gummy worms. "Sure you don't want any?" she asked.

"Mint chip and gummy worms – interesting combo. I don't think so," said Gertrude. Then she paused. "Well, maybe I'll have just a little ice cream. Ice cream is my one weakness."

"Good decision," said Zibby, giving her a scoop, "even if you *are* missing the best part!" She cheerfully bit the head off a gummy worm.

The two sat down at the kitchen table and Zibby spread the journal out along with some colored pencils and scrap paper.

"Since the book is about a boy and his two dogs," said Zibby, "I figure I should illustrate the pages with pictures of dogs. But every time I draw one, it just looks like a blob with legs."

"Here's a real easy way to draw dogs," said Gertrude.

She showed Zibby how to draw rectangles for the head and body, how to round out the lines to make them look not so square, and then how to add the legs.

When Zibby tried herself, she was amazed. "It doesn't look half bad," she said. "If I keep practicing, I think I can make some dog-like dogs! Now, Miss Cannon also said the pages of the journal have to look old – how the heck do I do that?"

"That's easy – just make some black tea, let it cool, then dip the pages in the tea to stain them. Once the pages dry, they'll look old and weathered," said Gertrude.

"Wow, you're a genius!" said Zibby.

"I've just done a lot of art projects," said Gertrude.

"Hey, that reminds me, I really want to see your award-winning painting," said Zibby.

Gertrude blinked. "What?" she asked.

"Your painting that won that big award – I'd like to see it," she repeated.

"Oh yeah," said Gertrude. "I can bring it to school on Monday if you want."

"That would be great – just don't forget," said Zibby.

"I won't," said Gertrude. "I promise."

After Gertrude went home later that day, Sarah called Zibby to ask how her journal was going.

"Awesome!" said Zibby. "Gertrude came over and helped me with my drawings and told me this really cool way to make the pages look old using tea. So I'm all set! I'm not worried at all anymore."

She was expecting Sarah to congratulate her, but instead she asked in a funny voice, "So Gertrude went over to your house?"

"Yeah, and she was so nice and helpful and she never once mentioned how great things were back where she used to live. And she wasn't even picky about what she ate! She's not as bad as you thought, really – you should give her another chance."

"I can't believe you didn't ask *me* to help you," Sarah said. "I could have helped you with your drawings, and I know how to make pages look old too."

Zibby hadn't thought of asking Sarah because she knew Sarah was busy with her own journal. "Gertrude asked me, and since she didn't have a journal to do, I said yes," she explained.

"I would have helped you anyway. That's what best friends are for," said Sarah. "Plus ... " her voice trailed off.

"What?" asked Zibby.

"You know I don't like her!" Sarah spat out suddenly. "I can't believe you spent all afternoon with her and didn't even call me!"

"Wow, I'm sorry, Sarah. I didn't know that would ... " Zibby started to say, but then Sarah said she had to go, and the line went dead. And suddenly, Zibby didn't feel so happy about her journal anymore.

CHAPTER 7

LUNCH FOR TWO ... OR THREE

When Zibby saw Sarah at school on Monday on the blacktop, she decided to pretend like everything was normal, which she was hoping it was.

"Hey, how's your journal going?" Zibby asked in a Super Cheerful voice.

"Fine," answered Sarah.

"Did you age the pages yet? That tea stain really works – I already did mine."

"I smudged dirt on mine – there are other ways to age pages, Zibby," Sarah said. "Even though I know Gertrude is *the big art expert.*"

"Um," Zibby stuttered, not knowing what to say. She guessed Sarah was still angry at her for having Gertrude over, even though she hadn't meant to do anything wrong. On the other hand, she didn't like having Sarah mad at her, so she offered a Supreme Sacrifice to make it up to her.

"How about if we hang out together at lunch today?" Zibby asked.

"Really?" Sarah brightened. But then she asked, "What about soccer?"

"I can always do that – you choose what we do today."

"Great – we can play mancala then," she said. Sarah loved all old-fashioned games like mancala and jacks. Zibby only tolerated them, but she was happy to play for Sarah's sake.

At lunch, Zibby sat down at a table and waited for Sarah to get through the cafeteria line. As she was waiting, Gertrude walked over to her carrying a big black case.

"What's that?" Zibby asked.

"My portfolio – with the painting you wanted to see."

"Oh yeah," said Zibby, remembering too late that she'd forgotten she'd asked to see Gertrude's art today. How would Sarah react when she saw her with Gertrude? *Oh well*, she figured, *it should only take a minute*. She couldn't very well tell Gertrude she didn't want to see her painting when she'd only brought it because Zibby had asked her to.

Gertrude opened up the portfolio and turned to a painting of what looked like a blue ocean with different shapes colored yellow, black, orange, and white floating in it. Or maybe it was a sky filled with shapes. But Zibby *could* tell one thing – it was good, really good.

"That's amazing," said Zibby. "Whatever it is! Like I said, I'm an art dummy!"

"It's an abstract," said Gertrude. "You know, where things don't look like they do in real life."

Zibby examined the painting more closely. "Is this ... a copy?" she asked.

"Oh – yes," said Gertrude. "The original is a lot bigger and is hanging up."

"Where?" asked Zibby.

"Oh, in ... my parents' house ... in the living room over the couch. So everyone can see it."

"Wow," said Zibby. "The only thing my parents ever displayed of mine was a clay vase I made in kindergarten. When my mom put water in it, the vase leaked all over her antique table and stained it permanently."

Just then Sarah appeared at the table, carrying her tray. When she saw Gertrude, her face fell.

"What's up?" Sarah asked in a wary voice.

"I'm just looking at Gertrude's painting," said Zibby guiltily. "It's the one she got the big award for."

"Oh," said Sarah, glancing down at the painting. "It's nice ... but it sort of looks familiar. I think I've seen it before."

"How could you have?" asked Gertrude with what Zibby thought was a little edge to her voice.

"I don't know," shrugged Sarah. "I guess I couldn't have. You know, I once won an art contest too. Kramer's Market had this coloring contest, and I colored a beach scene and it won. They even featured it in one of their ads."

"Nice ... but coloring isn't exactly art," said Gertrude.

"It's still an honor – like 500 kids entered the contest," said Sarah huffily.

"I'm sure it was a *big* honor," said Gertrude, closing her portfolio.

"Are you making fun of me?" asked Sarah.

"No, not at all," protested Gertrude.

"Yeah, right," said Sarah. "Other people can be good

artists too, you know."

"I never said they couldn't," said Gertrude.

Sarah didn't say anything else. She just shrugged her shoulders as if she didn't care about the conversation anymore. She then pulled out the mancala board from her backpack.

"Ready to play, Zibby?" she asked, ignoring Gertrude.

"Um, sure," said Zibby half-heartedly. Her special lunch with Sarah was already wrecked, what with the fighting between Sarah and Gertrude. And now she felt bad leaving out Gertrude so rudely, despite what she'd promised Sarah. So the next thing she knew, she blurted out to Gertrude, "Do you want to play too?"

Sarah's face dropped and she shot Zibby a "How could you do this?" look while Gertrude smiled at her gratefully.

"You're sure?" she asked, sitting down on one side of Zibby.

"Of course," said Zibby – even though she actually wasn't sure about anything at all right about now!

The girls started playing, but a layer of tension sat over them like their own personal black cloud. Zibby tried to think of a way to break the mood, which she could only describe as Awkward & Uncomfortable, when she was struck with one of her Very Good Ideas.

"Hey, you guys, you should hear this," Zibby said, pulling out her iPod from her backpack. "I just downloaded this CD called *Across the Universe* and it's really awesome. It's other artists singing Beatles songs."

"Sounds rad," said Gertrude.

"Cool," said Sarah, grabbing for one of the earbuds and sticking it in her ear. "I really want to hear it!"

Zibby turned on the iPod but hesitated when it came to putting the other earbud into her own ear. Too late, she realized her plan had a flaw – a big one. There were only two earbuds for the iPod, and there were three girls who wanted to listen! And she couldn't even offer the other earbud to Gertrude if she wanted to because the distance between Sarah and Gertrude was too big.

Slowly she put in the earbud, looking over at Gertrude to see how she was reacting.

"Whatever," said Gertrude, frowning and staring at the mancala board.

Zibby bit her lip and tried to get absorbed in the game, but it was nearly impossible because all she could think about was how they were leaving Gertrude out.

As soon as the first song, "All My Loving," was over, Zibby started to take out her earbud. But Sarah grabbed her arm and said, "Zibby, let's listen to the next song."

Oh no, thought Zibby, feeling now even *more* awkward about leaving out Gertrude. But she didn't have to feel awkward for much longer. Because the next thing she knew, Gertrude stood up and said, "That's it! Since you two are busy, I'm out of here," and she grabbed her portfolio and quickly walked away.

Sarah gave a little smile, but Zibby felt miserable. How was she ever going to be friends with *both* Sarah and Gertrude? Right now, it seemed impossible!

CHAPTER 8

MALL MADNESS

"Wait, Gertrude," Zibby yelled, following her. "I'm sorry – if only iPods came with three earphones," she said apologetically. In fact, she was thinking, the whole world was stacked against the number three – from earbuds to love seats to bicycles built for two to anything you needed a partner for!

"Well they don't," said Gertrude crossly.

"I'm sorry," Zibby said again.

"It's not really your fault," she said. "It's Sarah's. She's so possessive of you – how can you stand it?"

"Um," stammered Zibby, caught off guard. Maybe Sarah *was* being a bit possessive lately, but she didn't want to say anything bad about her.

"I really love your painting," said Zibby, changing the topic. "And we'll listen to *Across the Universe* together soon, I promise,"

"Sounds good," said Gertrude, softening.

"See you in class," said Zibby, heading back over to the lunch table to grab her iPod.

Sarah was stuffing the mancala game into her backpack. "Nice lunch we had, just the two of us," she said, angrily.

"I'm sorry," said Zibby. She was sure saying that a

lot today.

Sarah shrugged.

Then Zibby got another Very Good Idea. About how to make up to Sarah for the lunch for two that had turned out to be for three. And maybe how to salvage this whole Gertrude versus Sarah situation. She'd start only doing things one-on-one with each girl. And she had the perfect "alone" activity for her and Sarah that day.

"My mom's taking me to the mall after school today to go shopping for new T-shirts – want to come with me?" Zibby asked.

Sarah brightened. "I'll just check with my mom, but I think she'll say yes – thanks, Zibby," she smiled. And suddenly Zibby felt better – a lot better.

* * *

"Is this dress me or what?" asked Zibby, grabbing a slinky black dress off of a clothing rack later that afternoon. She and Sarah were talking to each other over the blaring music at a discount chain called "Cheap Thrills," which was crammed with clothes of all different styles. Her mom had dropped the girls off there while she and Zibby's three-year-old brother Sam went to the toy store.

"Totally! I can just see you at some fancy dance – tomboy goes glam!" laughed Sarah.

"As if!" Zibby put the dress back and then wandered over to a rack of T-shirts. Zibby picked up a striped white and blue T-shirt. "Now this is more like it," she said.

"You and your T-shirts," smiled Sarah. "I'm going to check out the dresses."

Even though they were best friends, Zibby and Sarah had opposite tastes in clothes. Zibby spent her life avoiding dresses, while Sarah wore one almost every day – the frillier, the better.

Zibby was standing at the T-shirt rack, when suddenly, who was standing right in front of her looking through a rack of scarves, but Gertrude! She couldn't believe it! What were the chances? She didn't mind running into Gertrude, but she knew Sarah would. And now her plan to get some alone time with Sarah was going down the drain!

"What – what are you doing here?" Zibby cried out.

Gertrude broke into a big smile when she saw her, then rushed over to Zibby. "Killing time while my mom's looking at lamps. What about you?"

"I'm here with Sarah, getting some T-shirts," said Zibby.

And as if on cue, Sarah came walking up to them with a Super Cranky Face.

"*You're* here?" she said, staring at Gertrude.

"Yep, I'm shopping with my mom."

"Oh, well, I'm here because Zibby invited *me* to go shopping with her," said Sarah, and she took a step closer to Zibby.

Great, thought Zibby. She *would* have to tell Gertrude that.

"Have you bought anything yet?" Zibby asked Gertrude

to get them onto another topic.

"No, but they sure have a lot of stuff crammed in here," said Gertrude, looking around. "And the music's so loud. At home we didn't have big malls like this. We just had little specialty stores that played classical or jazz music."

Sarah shook her head, and Zibby could just hear her saying to herself, "Not that stuff about how great it is at home again." Just then, a hip-hop song came on, and Sarah smiled and grabbed Zibby's arm.

"Hey, Zibby, does this remind you of something?" she asked. "Let's do the Funky Donkey!"

Sarah broke into the steps of a hip hop routine she'd learned in dance class that had been the unexpected hit of a party Zibby threw earlier in the year – unexpected since the girl who had led the dance was the weirdest girl in the class, Vanessa Heartgabel.

"Hee haw!" yelled Zibby, joining in as she and Sarah grapevined to the left, then spun around and shook their rear ends.

"Is that really a dance?" Gertrude asked skeptically.

"It sure is," said Sarah. "The Funky Donkey is one of the best ever, and we had so much fun doing it at Zibby's party. I guess you had to be there." She spun around again and yelled "Hee haw."

"I guess so," said Gertrude, crossing her arms and looking unhappy.

Zibby immediately quit dancing. "I'll teach it to you if you want," she said, trying to include Gertrude.

"No thanks," said Gertrude as she wandered off toward a rack of scarves.

"I guess since no one does it *back home*, she's not interested," Sarah rolled her eyes as she finished up the dance.

Zibby, however, didn't want to talk about Gertrude behind her back, so she drifted over to a rack against the wall and began looking through more T-shirts. She was trying to find something simple enough to meet with her tomboy approval when Sarah ran over, holding a yellow dress covered with sunflowers.

"This is adorable, don't you think?" asked Sarah.

"Cute," smiled Zibby, but the dress was so bright and girly, inside she couldn't help but think "Yuck," even though, of course, she'd never ever say such a thing to Sarah.

Gertrude, however, who had wandered back over to them, wasn't quite as tactful. "You're trying *that* on?" she asked Sarah.

"Yes, is something wrong?" asked Sarah.

"It's just a bit nerdy, don't you think?" asked Gertrude.

"No!" said Sarah in an insulted tone. "I think it's pretty."

"I just wonder if you'd really ever wear it once you got it home," continued Gertrude.

"Of course I would," said Sarah. "And I'm going to try it on right now!" She stormed off to the dressing room.

Once they were alone, Gertrude turned to Zibby and asked, "I was just trying to stop her from buying something she'd regret. Is she always so sensitive?"

Zibby sighed. "No," she said loyally.

A few minutes later, Sarah appeared with the dress on.

"It fits perfectly, and I'm getting it," she said, looking right at Gertrude. "Despite what you think."

"I don't think anything," Gertrude protested. "It looks rad on you, totally rad."

"Quit making fun of me!" Sarah snapped. "Plus, that word you keep using – rad – is really bugging me!"

"Now you don't like the way I talk?" asked Gertrude.

"Just like you don't like the way I dress," said Sarah.

"You're just being sensitive," said Gertrude.

"And you're being rude – I guess that's how you got your name – Gert-RUDE," said Sarah.

"Oh, good one. Well, now I think *you're* being rude," said Gertrude.

"I am not – am I, Zibby?" Sarah looked at Zibby expectantly.

"Yes, she is. Right, Zibby?" asked Gertrude.

"What?" said Zibby, stalling for time and thinking, *Don't drag me into this, please!*

"Tell her," ordered Sarah.

"Tell *her*," said Gertrude.

But Zibby just stood there, knowing that whatever she said would make one of them mad, when suddenly, an idea popped into her brain.

"Funky Donkey everyone!" she yelled, twirling around, wiggling her rear, and yelling, "Hee haw." But when she turned around, all she saw were the angry faces of Gertrude and Sarah. This time, not even Sarah was dancing.

CHAPTER 9

SOME REALLY GOOD BAD ADVICE

"Boy, that was fun – not!" Zibby said to herself about the trip to the mall when she got home later. Luckily for her, just after her Failed Funky Donkey Distraction, Gertrude had to go, so Zibby never did have to choose between one of the girls. She and Sarah were able to finish their shopping in peace.

But still, her plan to get some quality time with Sarah had been spoiled, which made her question the entire idea of trying to spend separate time with Gertrude and Sarah in the first place. If she couldn't even avoid having them run into each other at the mall, how could she stop the three of them from running into each other all the time at school, especially since they were in the same class?

If only she could split herself into two Zibbys – one could hang out with Sarah, the other with Gertrude. But sadly, Zibby-cloning hadn't been discovered yet!

This is a big mess, the biggest friendship mess ever, she thought – which was saying a lot because she'd run into pretty big ones before. *What am I going to do?*

* * *

At recess the next day she was surprised to find that her feet felt heavy and that somehow the idea of playing soccer seemed as if it was too much of an effort. On impulse, she ducked into the nurse's office. The nurse was hardly ever there because she had to rotate between all the schools in the city. So Zibby figured she could sit on the cot in solitude until she figured out what to do about the Terrible Case of her TFFs – Two Feuding Friends.

When she walked into the office, she was surprised to see Amber sitting at the nurse's desk, sipping on a smoothie.

"How come *you're* here?" Zibby asked, sitting down on the cot.

"I come in here sometimes for a little 'me' time when the nurse isn't around." Amber put her drink down and applied some Groovy Grapilicious lip gloss.

"Where'd you get the smoothie?" asked Zibby.

"My mom brought it. I missed breakfast," said Amber. "She brings me one whenever I don't have time to eat before school."

Wow, thought Zibby, *the only thing I get when I don't have time to eat my Cheerios is a growling stomach.*

"So what's wrong with *you*?" asked Amber. "You don't have the flu, do you?" she leaned away from Zibby as if Zibby had contracted some type of flesh-eating disease.

"No, I'm just kind of stressed," she said.

"Oh," Amber relaxed in her chair now that she knew Zibby wasn't contagious. "About what?" she asked.

Zibby hesitated. She didn't really feel like confiding in

Amber, but on the other hand, she felt like if she didn't talk about her dilemma, she might burst.

"So Gertrude – " Zibby started to say, but Amber interrupted.

"You know, I checked out some of those pre-loved clothes online that she was talking about, and I'm going to order some. I luv them," she gushed.

"Well, anyway," Zibby continued, not wanting to talk about Amber's latest fashion finds, "we've become friends and I really like her. But Sarah doesn't like Gertrude. And Gertrude doesn't like Sarah. They fight all the time and talk about each other to me, and I don't know what to do!"

"Maybe they're just frenemies," said Amber.

"What the heck is that?" yelled Zibby. Lately it seemed as if Amber spoke a whole other language.

"You know – they sort of like each other, sort of hate each other."

Zibby thought for a moment. "I think they're more like ... plain old enemies," she concluded.

"Oh," Amber nodded, taking another slurp of her drink. "They're going green on ya then," she said knowingly.

"What?" asked Zibby. "You mean, like environmentally friendly?"

"Come on, Zibby," Amber rolled her eyes. "Like in the green-eyed monster – jealousy. Are they, like, fighting over *you*? It happens to me all the time. Everyone wants to be one of my peeps, but there's not enough Amber to go around for everybody!" She smiled and shrugged her shoulders as if to say it wasn't her fault she was so fabulous.

"Yeah, I guess they are jealous," admitted Zibby, even though it felt almost stuck-up to admit it.

"Then there's only one thing to do," said Amber definitively. "Choose one."

"What do you mean?" asked Zibby.

"Make your choice. You're either Sarah's friend or your Gertrude's friend. Then you dump the other one. Problem solved."

"But I don't want to chose," Zibby protested. "Sarah's been my best friend forever and I love her. And I really like Gertrude, and it's fun to have a new friend. Plus, I'm her only real friend here. I can't dump either of them."

"Good luck," said Amber. "Having fighting friends is a real drag – it's not going to get any better."

Zibby just sat there, looking miserable.

"Or, if you don't want to choose between them, dump them both!" Amber said. "That way you don't have to choose. If your old BFF and your new BFF don't like each other, it's time to get some new BFFs."

"But I don't want new BFFS!" yelled Zibby.

"Yep, that's my friendship diagnosis. You need some new peeps in your life." Amber stood up and gave a big smile as if she hadn't heard what Zibby had said. "That's it. That's your solution. I'm so good, I should charge for this." She chucked her empty smoothie container in the trash and started to leave the room. "Next time, it's gonna cost you."

Wow, Amber sure was a big help, thought Zibby sarcastically. *As if I'd ever pay a penny for advice from her.*

But then, when she reflected on what Amber had said, she realized that in a way, Amber *had* helped: Amber made her realize there was no way she could choose between Sarah and Gertrude. She wanted to keep them both as friends. She had to save these friendships. They both meant too much to her!

And then, she was hit with the Absolute Best Idea. Because, to use Amber's words, if her new BFF and her old BFF clashed, it wasn't time for *new* BFFs. It was time to help the new BFF and the old BFF *get along.*

"That's it," she said to herself. "All I have to do is get Sarah and Gertrude to like each other – then my problems will be over. I won't be stuck in the middle anymore and we can all be friends – a Big, Happy Group of Three!"

Forget separating the two girls – instead, she'd figure out ways to push them together! Then it would only be a matter of time before they started appreciating each other. Zibby smiled triumphantly.

The only problem now, she thought as her smile began to fade, *is how to go about doing it!*

CHAPTER 10

OPERATION FRIENDSHIP

For the rest of the day, Zibby pondered the question of how to bring Sarah and Gertrude together. She couldn't think about anything else until she had a plan in place.

And by dinnertime she had one. A sure-fire plan that had to work. With a sure-fire name, too: "Operation Friendship," she whispered fiercely to herself as she set the table, "will launch – tonight!"

She called Sarah and arranged to meet her at 3:30 after school the next day at the local ice cream shop, The Scoop. Then she called Gertrude and told her to meet her at the same place at the same time. Now all she had to do was wait until tomorrow, when she knew she'd score a Total Friendship Victory between the two girls!

* * *

The next day after school, Zibby hurried over to The Scoop at 3:20. No one was in the ice cream parlor except for her older brother Anthony's friend Torrance who worked behind the counter.

"Hey, Tor, I need your help," she said.

"Yeah?" he grunted.

"Can you let me hide behind the counter – I swear I won't get in your way," she asked. She then quickly made up a story for why she was hiding, because the truth seemed too embarrassing. "I'm doing a science project and I want to see if I can guess from the tone of people's voice what kind of ice cream they will order. Research shows that tone of voice is very revealing when it comes to ice cream choice."

"Yeah? Cool," said Torrance. "Come on around."

"Great – I'll hide here," she said, scooting behind the counter and crouching down beneath the ice cream tubs.

Just then, she heard the door open. She ducked her head down and waited.

"Welcome to The Scoop, where we scoop 'em large, we scoop 'em small, we scoop 'em any way at all," said Torrance in a quick monotone. "Which of our awesome 29 flavors would you prefer?"

"None yet, thanks. I'm waiting for Zibby," a voice said. It was Sarah.

"Dude, she's right ... " Torrance started to say when Zibby hit him across the back of the knee again.

"Ow!" yelled Torrance.

"Shhhh," Zibby whispered, putting her fingers on her lips. "I'm not here, remember?"

"Sorry," he whispered down to her, then looked back out across the counter.

"Everything okay?" Sarah asked Torrance.

"Uh, yeah," said Torrance, rubbing the back of his leg.

Then Zibby heard another person enter the shop.

"Welcome to the Scoop, where we scoop 'em large, we scoop 'em small, we scoop 'em any way at all," repeated Torrance. "Which of our awesome 29 flavors would you prefer?"

But the person didn't answer. The next thing Zibby heard was Gertrude, asking in a raised voice, "What are you doing here?"

"I'm meeting Zibby," Sarah answered. "What about *you*?"

"*I'm* meeting Zibby. She didn't say *you'd* be here," said Gertrude.

"Well, she didn't mention *you*, either."

"You must have gotten mixed up," said Gertrude.

"I don't think so – I think you're the one who got mixed up," said Sarah. "I'm going to call her right now."

But Zibby had purposely turned off her cell phone so she couldn't be reached.

"No answer," said Sarah. "Where is she?"

"On her way to meet me here, probably," said Gertrude.

"You mean on her way to meet *me*," snapped Sarah.

No, no, no, Zibby was thinking. This wasn't going the way she'd planned. They weren't supposed to be arguing, they were supposed to be using this "alone" time to bond with each other without Zibby around. Plus everyone's always happy in an ice cream shop, aren't they? At least Zibby was. And, ice cream was the one "junk food" Gertrude would eat. And The Scoop had so many killer flavors.

Maybe, she realized, if they actually ate some ice cream,

they'd get in better moods and start getting along. She hit Torrance in the back of the knee.

"Ow!" he yelled, then bent down to Zibby's level. "Now what?" he asked.

"Sorry, but listen, have them order! Right now!" she whispered.

"For your science project?" he whispered back.

"Yes," she hissed.

He stood back up. "Girls, while you wait, why don't you have some ice cream," he suggested.

"Well, I *am* hungry," said Sarah. "I'll have a double scoop of vanilla on a cake cone, please."

"Vanilla?" asked Gertrude with a touch of disapproval.

"What's wrong with that?" asked Sarah.

"Vanilla is so ... boring!" exclaimed Gertrude. "Come on, they have '29 awesome flavors!'"

"Vanilla happens to be the most popular ice cream in the world," says Sarah. "Only boring people think it's boring."

"Well, that can't be true because I'm certainly not boring."

"So what exciting flavor are *you* getting?" Sarah asked as Torrance handed her the cone and she paid. "Oh wait, you probably don't even eat ice cream, do you?"

"Hmm," Gertrude considered, not responding to Sarah's last statement. Then she asked Torrance, "Do you have any sugar-free flavors?"

"Nope," said Torrance.

"Organic?"

"Nope."

"Soy-based?"

"Nope," said Torrance. "Look, this is just a normal ice cream joint. Not one of those weirdo health food places."

"Nothing, then," said Gertrude. "I don't eat just *normal* ice cream."

What's going on? Zibby asked herself. Gertrude ate ice cream with her just the other day and it wasn't sugar-free, soy, or organic. Why wouldn't she eat it today?

But she didn't have time to think about Gertrude's on-again off-again taste for ice cream because the next thing she knew, the girls were back to arguing.

"You don't eat ice cream?" asked Sarah. "You *are* the boring one."

"I am not. I just care about what goes into *my* body," said Gertrude.

"You think you're so much better than everyone," exploded Sarah. "But you know what ... " she started to say when Torrance interrupted her.

"Dudes, no bad vibes inside The Scoop," Torrance reprimanded them. "This is a family place. If you two are going to get all snarly with each other, take it outside."

"Yeah, Sarah, I don't need any more of your bad vibes. I'm gone!" said Gertrude.

Zibby heard the shuffling of feet and the door opening and closing.

"I'm going too," said Sarah to Torrance. Zibby heard more shuffling, then another slam of the door.

Zibby waited about a minute more, then popped up to

see what was happening out on the street. There was Sarah striding off in one direction, and Gertrude going off in the opposite one.

"Did ya get enough info for your science project?" Torrance asked her.

"Oh, yeah, I got enough all right," she said bitterly. She got more than enough information to know that Operation Friendship had been a big fat flop!

She sat down at a table, feeling crushed. But not so crushed she didn't order something to eat – a mint chip sundae with extra gummy worms. As she sat there, chewing on the worms, however, she began to rebound.

"I can't give up after only one try," she said to herself. "There's got to be another way to get them to become friends."

She thought about one time earlier in the year when she and Sarah weren't getting along and Sarah had sent her a pair of green high-tops as a peace offering. That had turned everything around and they made up after that.

Thinking back to that incident, Zibby began to smile. Because now she knew what she was going to do for Phase II of Operation Friendship. And this time – she gulped down the last gummy worm in determination – her plan was absolutely going to be a success!

CHAPTER 11

A DECEITFUL RECEIPT

"The first thing I need to do is apologize!" Zibby said to herself as she left The Scoop. She whipped out her cell phone and dialed first Gertrude and then Sarah. She quickly said she'd gotten mixed-up, then hung up before they could ask a lot of questions.

The next step of Phase II: Beg her mom to take her to the local health food store.

There, she picked out an item from the bakery section, then went home and transferred it to a paper plate and covered it in plastic wrap. Next, she waded into her Very Cluttered Closet and after looking through piles of discarded stuff from over the years, she found what she was looking for and wrapped it up. *Nice*, Zibby thought as she admired Phase II of her plan. She was convinced that *she* would soon be crowned the "friendship genius," not Amber.

At school the next day, she eagerly stood out on the blacktop, waiting for Sarah and Gertrude. She saw Gertrude first and sprinted over to her, digging something out of her backpack.

"This is for *yooou*," Zibby sang out, taking a plate of muffins out of her backpack.

"I was talking to Sarah about yesterday, and she told me she's really sorry you two aren't getting along. So sorry in fact that she wanted me to give you this present: Homemade fat-free muffins made with love. It took her hours to bake them." Zibby ripped the plastic wrap off the muffins and thrust them at Gertrude.

In reality, these muffins were the ones that Zibby bought yesterday at the health food store, but she figured Gertrude would never know.

"Really?" Gertrude looked suspicious.

"And you don't even have to thank her – don't even mention it to her. Just enjoy the homemade muffins," said Zibby.

"That's nice of her," said Gertrude, looking less skeptical.

"I know – isn't it? She is such a thoughtful person," said Zibby.

She was about to compliment Sarah some more, but just then she saw Sarah enter the blacktop.

"Gotta go. *Bon appétit!*" she yelled out to Gertrude as she hurried over to Sarah.

"Hey, Sarah, look what I have for you from Gertrude." Out of her backpack she whipped out the item she'd found in her closet and wrapped – a magnet craft set someone had given her years ago that she'd never used. "She says she's sorry she has been so rude and she wants you to have this to make up for it."

"For real?" Sarah asked.

"For real!" nodded Zibby.

Sarah quickly ripped off the wrapping paper, and smiled when she saw the crafts set.

"That was nice of her. I guess she's not *all* bad if she can apologize."

"Of course she's not!" exclaimed Zibby. "She's really nice. I keep telling you that. And she says you don't even have to thank her. Don't even mention the gift! Just have fun with it."

"I will," said Sarah.

"Yippee!" Zibby thought to herself as she ran over to stand in line where her class lined up on the blacktop. "This is actually working. *I am* the friendship genius. Now we can all be friends and my troubles will be over!"

But the next thing Zibby knew, Gertrude was walking over to her, carrying a crumpled piece of white paper in her hand.

"You'll never guess what I found!" Gertrude said. "A receipt" – she waved the piece of paper in front of Zibby's face – "for the *homemade* muffins. When I took off the plastic wrap to try one, *this* was stuck to the bottom of the plate!"

How'd that get there? Zibby groaned to herself. She should have been more careful when she transferred the cookies from the grocery bag to the plate. That receipt was blowing everything!

"One box fat-free muffins, $6.99," Gertrude read from the receipt out loud. "So it took Sarah hours to bake these, huh? I don't think so!"

"I'm sure that's from something else," said Zibby, grabbing the receipt out of Gertrude's hand and stuffing it into her pocket.

"Right," said Gertrude. "She just happened to buy some muffins the exact same day she made them for me. I didn't know Sarah was a liar on top of everything else."

"She's not – she never lies!" protested Zibby. This was true. Sarah was the most honest person she'd ever met.

"Isn't it a lie when you tell someone you made them something and you really bought it?" persisted Gertrude.

"But it's not the same receipt – I'm telling you!" Zibby yelled.

"You just don't see her for what she is," said Gertrude, shaking her head.

Oh no, thought Zibby, *this is only making things worse! Well*, Zibby tried to cheer herself up, *at least Sarah liked the craft set.*

But then she saw Sarah walking quickly toward her and Gertrude, and she didn't look happy. At all. Zibby rushed up to meet her.

"Can you believe it?" Sarah asked her. "I looked at the instructions, and this craft set is for five-year-olds! I know what she's trying to say – that when it comes to art, I'm a baby."

Oh no, thought Zibby. *I should have checked out the craft set better before giving it to her!* "I'm sure that wasn't what she meant," Zibby started to explain, when she was interrupted by Gertrude, who'd followed her.

"Thanks for the *homemade muffins* – ha!" she said to Sarah.

"I don't know what you're talking about," said Sarah. "But I can thank *you* for this craft set – *for five-year-olds!*"

"What craft set?" asked Gertrude.

"Other people are artists, too, you know, even if we don't win big 'ol awards," said Sarah.

"Are you still hung up on that?" asked Gertrude. "I didn't mean to insult that little coloring contest you were in."

"Little? See? There you go again, putting it down."

"Well you were the one who brought it up," countered Gertrude.

Zibby plugged her ears and sat down on the blacktop, wishing she could disappear. Or at least make her gifts disappear – which she had to admit had gone even worse than Phase I of Operation Friendship!

The bell rang, which thankfully put an end to Sarah and Gertrude's fighting because they had to get in line and file into class. But nothing, it seemed to Zibby right then, would put an end to her friendship woes.

CHAPTER 12

A CRAFTY IDEA

"Why me?" Zibby cried out loud at lunchtime, even though no one was there to hear her. She was back in the nurse's room, which this time, thankfully, was empty so she could stew in privacy.

Everything she'd done had backfired! She was running out of ideas and patience. She wanted to have fun with Sarah and Gertrude, not waste all her time scheming up ways to get them to be friends – ways that never worked anyway!

She slumped down on the nurse's cot. How could she not have seen that receipt on the plate? Or why hadn't she just told Gertrude the muffins were store-bought in the first place? It still would have been a nice gesture. And why did she have to pick that one craft set when her closet was filled with much cooler ones – and ones for older kids – that she'd gotten more recently from far away relatives who never seemed to understand that she just wasn't into art.

Then, suddenly, thinking about her closet gave her another idea. One final way that might work to finally once and for all secure the success of Operation Friendship. She sat up and fleshed out a final Best Buddies or Bust Plan to push Sarah and Gertrude together.

That night, she sent each girl a separate text message saying they'd each won a prize. She asked Sarah to come to her house at 4:00 and Gertrude to come to her house at 4:15 the next day. Friday afternoon when she got home from school, she pulled out all the craft sets she could find in her closet, selected those that she felt Gertrude and Sarah would deem fun, put them in a pillow case, and then put the pillow case in the closet. Then she went outside and waited for the girls.

When Sarah arrived, Zibby quickly sent her up to her room, saying she'd be there in a few minutes. When Gertrude arrived fifteen minutes later, she escorted Gertrude up to her room as well.

"How come *she's* here?" Sarah gasped when she saw Gertrude.

"Yeah – what's going on?" Gertrude demanded, but Zibby ignored them both. She closed the door behind the three of them and stood in front of it like a guard.

"Just hear me out," said Zibby. "Please. Pretty please. Double, triple pretty please with extra gummy worms on top. Can you both just take a seat and listen to me?"

Sarah sighed and then sat down on Zibby's bed. Gertrude frowned then sat down on the floor.

"Thank you," said Zibby, relieved that at least this part of Phase III of Operation Friendship – getting Sarah and Gertrude together in one room – had worked.

"I called you both here today because as I said, I really

do have a prize for you both. And the prize is ... each other! This is your chance to get to know each other and become friends. Because I, for one, can't take being in the middle of your fighting anymore. I'm going crazy!"

"*This* is crazy," said Sarah, with a big grumpy frown on her face. Gertrude was staring at Zibby with her mouth open.

"You both love art, and I think working on some projects would bring you together," Zibby continued. "So here are some crafts – good ones, not baby ones."

She opened her closet door, grabbed the pillow case, and dumped the crafts out on the floor. "Have fun, and don't come out until you're friends."

"And oh," Zibby added. "Don't even *think* about leaving the room, because I've got a bodyguard outside to make sure you don't!" And with that, she slammed the door shut.

She really did have a bodyguard, even though he wasn't exactly what you'd call intimidating.

"Sam," she called to her little brother, whose room was right across the hall. "It's time – just like we talked about."

Sam toddled out of his room, holding a can of Silly String.

"Now, remember, if Sarah or Gertrude tries to come out, squirt them with this," she said.

"'Kay, 'Ibby," smiled Sam, who, even though he was only three, had very good aim when it came to Silly String slimings.

Sam had barely taken his position in front of the door

when Sarah pushed it open a few inches and peeked out, looking as if she was about to bolt.

"*Sssss!*" Sam glopped her with a direct hit of Silly String.

"Yuck!" screamed Sarah. "I hate that stuff – it stains everything," she said, quickly retreating and closing the door.

"Good work, Sam," smiled Zibby. "Keep it up and you'll get your reward – a whole dollar."

"Me richie," said Sam with a big grin.

"That's right – you'll be rich," Zibby nodded.

Zibby went into the TV room right next to her room and pulled out her math homework. She liked to be efficient and figured why not get her homework done at the same time she was running Operation Friendship. It was hard to concentrate, however, especially as she kept expecting to hear either fighting from inside her room or screams as Sam Silly-Stringed Gertrude or Sarah. And after about ten minutes of silence, she went out to the hallway to relieve Sam of his duty. If they hadn't tried to leave the room again yet, she figured they weren't going to. Plus, she didn't think Sam could last just standing there much longer.

"Good job," she said, digging into her pocket and handing him a dollar.

"Tanks," he smiled, then carefully walked down the stairs to find their mom.

Zibby smiled too. Her plan seemed to be working, so she went back into the TV room to do more homework. After awhile longer, however, she couldn't resist walking over and putting her ear to the door of her room. And just when she did, she heard a big yelp from inside.

"What's wrong?" she yelled, flinging open the door. "You two aren't fighting are you?"

But as soon as she took one look at the girls, she relaxed. They were sitting on the floor doing just what she'd hoped they'd do – they making crafts ... together!

"I just pricked my finger with this wire on the bead set," said Gertrude, holding out her index finger. "But I'm fine." She strung a bead onto a black wire.

"Wow," said Zibby, looking around the room, smiling again. "You're both getting along!"

"Yep," smiled Sarah. "At first we were kinda mad that you locked us up in here ... "

"I didn't lock you in," protested Zibby. "I had a three-year-old outside, come on!"

"Yeah – armed with gross Silly String!" said Sarah. "But anyway, then we realized it was actually kind of sweet."

"You must really care about us both to work so hard to get us to like each other," said Gertrude.

"Oh and we figured it all out – about The Scoop and about the presents we supposedly gave each other," said Sarah. "Zibby, you are so wacky sometimes."

"Wacky-good, though," said Gertrude, putting a final silver bead on her necklace and holding it up to her chest.

"That's beautiful, Trude," said Sarah.

"Trude?" asked Zibby, taken aback.

"That's what my friends back home sometimes called

me," said Gertrude.

"I didn't know that," said Zibby, wondering why she didn't know that.

She crouched down on the floor. "Anything for me to make – maybe there's a fake tattoo for my ankle?" she asked, pointing to a temporary tattoo making kit.

"Sorry – we made them all," said Gertrude, displaying an angel tattoo on the top of her hand.

"And look at my rad heart," said Sarah, showing off a tattoo on her forearm.

Rad? thought Zibby. Sarah sure was quick to pick up some Gertrudisms – even the one she had hated!

"Besides, you don't like stuff like this anyway, remember?" asked Sarah.

"Still, I thought, maybe I could do *something*," said Zibby.

"Actually you could do something to help us," said Gertrude. "Do you have a hot glue gun? I want to hot glue some of these miniature roses to the frame," she held up a frame decorated with pom poms and fabric, "but the glue that came in the craft set isn't strong enough."

"I think there's one downstairs," said Zibby, standing up. "I guess I can go get it."

"Thanks, Zibby," said Gertrude.

"Oh and Zibby ... " Sarah said. Zibby turned around.

"Woops – I meant Trude," laughed Sarah. "If we have the glue gun, then we can glue some of the roses to the purse we made."

"Rad idea!" nodded Gertrude.

"I'll just go get the glue gun now," said Zibby, but neither of them seemed to hear her.

And as she walked down the stairs she was hit with a curious emotion. She knew she should be thrilled that Operation Friendship had finally worked, but she didn't feel quite as ecstatic as she thought she would. After all her worrying about whether either Sarah or Gertrude was feeling left out, suddenly she was feeling a little left out herself.

CHAPTER 13

ODD GIRL OUT

Sarah and Gertrude stayed another half hour at Zibby's house finishing up the rest of the crafts. When they left, they couldn't thank Zibby enough.

"You are the best friend, ever," Sarah said as she gave Zibby a big hug. "I was so tired of all that fighting, and I really hadn't given Gertrude a chance. Thanks for bringing us together."

Gertrude was grateful too. "It was so rad what you did for us. You are one awesome peace maker."

"Thanks," said Zibby, wondering why, if she was such a good peace maker, she didn't feel very peaceful inside.

* * *

At school on Monday, Gertrude and Sarah entered the blacktop together arm in arm.

"You won't believe what Trude and I are going to do!" Sarah gushed as soon as she saw Zibby.

Zibby ignored Sarah's comment. She was curious about something else.

"Um, did you two walk to school together?" Zibby asked. She'd never seen them arrive at the exact same time before.

"Oh, yeah," replied Gertrude. "I just live a few blocks away from Sarah – on Linden Avenue – so I figured I'd walk on over this morning and pick her up."

Hmm, thought Zibby. *They could have stopped by my house to pick me up too. I live right on the way.*

And that's when she first felt it – a big stab of jealousy.

"Anyway, we were talking last night," Sarah started to say.

"You guys did something together last night?" asked Zibby.

"No, but we've been talking on the phone all weekend … including last night," said Sarah. "And anyway, the big news is, Gertrude's going to teach me how to knit!"

"Really?" said Zibby, trying not to sound horrified. She just couldn't imagine *anyone* getting excited about knitting. She'd seen her mom knit a sweater once and it looked like the most Painfully Boring Pastime on the Planet.

"Yeah – we're going to make these really rad ponchos everyone wears back home," said Gertrude.

"*Ahem*," Sarah cleared her throat playfully and gave Gertrude a knowing glance.

"Woops, sorry," said Gertrude. "I promised Sarah I wouldn't say that anymore. I didn't realize how annoying it was," she explained to Zibby. She looked thoughtful for a moment. "Hey, in fact, there's something I've been wanting to tell you guys ... "

But she never got a chance to finish her sentence because Sarah interrupted her. "Don't worry, Gertrude, it wasn't that annoying," she said reassuringly. Then she turned to Zibby. "Anyway, we're going to knit every recess and lunch – we'd ask you if you wanted to join us, but I know you'd rather play soccer."

"Oh," Zibby's face fell – and that's when she was hit with Jealousy Stab #2. Because even though Sarah was right – she didn't want to sit around getting all tangled up in yarn – at least they could have *asked* her if she'd wanted to join them.

But then, she scolded herself – she was being silly. This was what she wanted, after all – for Gertrude and Sarah to be friends. Her plan had worked. She should be feeling happy, not jealous.

"Have fun with your knitting fest," she said trying to sound more cheerful than she felt. "And I'll have fun out on the soccer field."

But at recess, when Zibby went to join the boys, she got a surprise.

"The soccer field's closed," announced Matthew, her soccer buddy and her past co-star of the school musical. "The sprinklers ran all night by mistake, and the grass is flooded. It may take all week to dry out and we can't play on it until then."

Oh no, thought Zibby. Not only would she miss playing

soccer, but now what was she going to do? Who would she hang out with?

Well, she continued to think, *I guess I'll just stay here ... and hang out with the boys anyway.*

"So hey," she said to the group, "What should we do now?"

"I dunno," one of the boys named Kyle mumbled, shuffling his feet.

"BURPING CONTEST!" yelled out another boy named Drew. He then took a big breath and let out a long, disgusting "BRRRRRP."

"Dude, that was foul," said Kyle.

"You're just jealous cuz your burps aren't as awesome," said Drew, letting out another big one.

"No way – listen to this," said Kyle. He took a deep breath, opened his mouth, and gave a small burp.

"That was weak," laughed Matthew. "A girl could burp better than that. Come on, you try, Zibby!"

"Yeah, let it rip, Zibby," urged Drew.

"No thank you," said Zibby firmly. She'd been through a burp infatuation stage earlier in the year and it wasn't any fun at all when she started burping when she didn't even mean to. If this was all the boys did – burp and make fun of each other – then she wasn't going to stick around.

Leaving the field, she saw Amber and her "peeps" sitting under the shade of a big pepper tree. Since hanging with the boys didn't work out, she figured she could give them a chance. After all, she used to be good friends with

Amber and Camille; she could use this time to renew her friendships with them. They must still have *something* in common, right?

But as she approached the group, she saw that the girls were huddled around another one of those teen magazines, *Celeb Chat* – *yuck*! But she was still determined to try with them, so she gave a big smile and said as cheerfully as possible, "Hi, everyone."

"Hey, Zibby," the girls said, then quickly bent their heads back down to the magazine – except for Amber, who asked, "So did you take my advice?"

"No," said Zibby.

Amber tossed her head. "Bad move," she smirked. "But, hey, it's your life."

"Yes, it is," said Zibby. So maybe her plan hadn't worked out the way she wanted, but it was still better than Amber's!

"By the way, I ordered some of those pre-loved clothes. They should be here any day," said Amber.

"That's nice," said Zibby politely, but inside she was thinking, *Who cares?*

Suddenly, Camille squealed. "Oh my gosh! Will you look at this picture?" She showed Zibby a photo of Fabrio lounging against a car. "He's so cute!"

"Mega cute," nodded one FOA – Friend of Amber's – named Savannah.

"Mega way cute," pronounced Amber.

"*Alpha omega* cute," said Zibby, smiling, making what

she thought was a clever word play off the name of a sorority she'd heard of on a TV show. But the girls just stared at her as if she'd just said the stupidest thing ever.

"There is no *alpha omega cute*," said Amber. "Come on, Zibby!"

"And, get this," Camille squealed, still wrapped up in the magazine. "This article says he just broke up with his girlfriend, Jazmeena, so he's available!"

"Who's Jazmeena?" asked Zibby.

"Where've you been, Zibby? Living under a giant soccer ball?" asked Amber. "She's only the best-selling pop artist right now!"

"Well, excuse me," said Zibby just as the class bell rang.

Hallelujah, she thought. She didn't think she could last much longer with Amber & Company anyway!

As she headed over to class, she saw Gertrude and Sarah on the other side of hall. They were sharing an iPod and were admiring some bright yellow yarn as they walked. She gave them a wave, but they were so absorbed in the music and the yarn, they didn't even look up. She waved even harder, with both of her hands, but they still didn't see her. It was as if they were in their own little universe.

This is just great, Zibby thought. *The next thing I know they'll be swapping shoes, doing the secret greeting, and knitting entire matching wardrobes together.*

She'd wanted so much for it to be "S, Z & G," a Happy Group of Three, but instead, she'd wound up being Zibby

Payne, Unhappy Group of One – and even worse, it was all by her own doing!

"Zibby Payne," she scolded herself as so many others had done in her lifetime, now finally understanding why they said it, "you can be a pain – a really big one!"

CHAPTER 14

VISIT TO GERTRUDE'S HOUSE

The rest of the week Zibby tried hanging out with a few other kids, but she didn't have fun with them either. And every time she ran into Sarah and Gertrude, they looked as if they were having the time of their lives while she, Zibby, was having the worst time ever!

"What if I lose Sarah for good – and Gertrude, too?" Zibby asked herself on Friday night as she sat on her bed, trying to cheer herself up by listening to the Eagles, but having no success. She could just see herself, Lonely Zibby, destined to wander through the halls of Lincoln Elementary all alone, forever.

And that's when she made her decision. One she'd never make in a million years if she weren't feeling so abandoned. "I'm going to learn to knit!" she declared. "It's the only way to get Sarah and Gertrude back."

On Saturday morning, she called both girls to see if she could join them for a "fun" weekend of knitting pearls and dropping puns, or whatever the heck the correct terms were, but neither girl answered her cell phone. No one answered the phone at Sarah's house either. So, she decided to drop by Gertrude's house and see if the girls were there. She didn't have Gertrude's home phone number, but she remembered Gertrude had said she lived on Linden Avenue. She knew where that was, so she headed over.

When she arrived on Linden, she saw a Prius parked out front of a green two-story house.

"This must be it," Zibby said to herself.

Zibby rang the doorbell, and a tall woman with brown hair answered.

"Mrs. Long?" she asked and the woman nodded. "I'm Zibby – one of Gertrude's friends. I'm trying to find Gertrude and Sarah."

"Oh, Zibby," Mrs. Long said as she smiled widely. "I've been wanting to meet you. You've been such a good friend to Gertrude."

"Thanks," smiled Zibby. "So are they here?"

"I'm sorry, honey, no. Gertrude ran down to the knitting store in town to meet Sarah."

Zibby knew where the store was – her mom had dragged here there once – and figured she'd go meet them when Mrs. Long asked, "Why don't you come on in for a minute and have a snack before you go. I'd hate for you to have come all the way over here for nothing."

"Oh, no thanks, I don't want to bother you – " Zibby started to say, when she changed her mind. Actually, it might be pretty interesting to see Gertrude's kitchen and what kind of super healthy, organically friendly snacks Mrs. Long served. "Well ... sure, okay," she said. "That's really nice of you."

She stepped inside the Longs' house and into the living room. Hanging over the couch was a picture of a bowl of fruit. "So is this the painting Gertrude won a big award for?" she asked, even though as she asked the question, she realized it didn't look at all like the painting Gertrude had shown her.

"What?" Mrs. Long said, crinkling her forehead. "Gertrude's a good artist, but she's never won a big award. Not yet, at least! But her last art teacher did like this pretty little still life she did. Just follow me into the kitchen."

"Um, sure," Zibby said a little confused. *Oh well*, she thought, *there must be some explanation. Or maybe I misunderstood what Gertrude had said.*

Once in the kitchen, Mrs. Long opened up a cabinet drawer, then turned to Zibby. "What would you like to eat? Some chips? A granola bar? Maybe some fruit strips?"

"You eat that stuff?" Zibby yelled out. What was Mrs. Long doing offering her the very same "junk food" Gertrude said she didn't eat?

"Is something wrong? Are you on a special diet or something?" asked Mrs. Long, looking concerned.

"Oh no," Zibby said, trying to calm down. "I just thought that Gertrude only ate health food."

"Gertrude?" Mrs. Long laughed. "She eats her share of salads and apples, but she does love her snack food. She even bought some Cheetos the other day if you want some."

Cheetos? Zibby's mouth dropped open. But she then quickly tried to regain her composure.

"Sure, I love Cheetos. Thank you."

Mrs. Long poured a few into a bowl and set them down on the kitchen table next to a big coffee table book. "Have a seat, honey," she said.

Zibby sat down, wondering, *What's going on?* She needed more time to think about all this, but Mrs. Long stood across from her and looked at her expectantly. Zibby, remembering her manners, did her best to make polite chit chat.

"So I hear Mr. Long's an artist too," Zibby said.

"I guess, if you consider house painting artistic, which it can be," she answered.

"He's a house painter?" Zibby asked, almost gagging on the Cheetos.

"Yes, why? Do your parents need one? He moved down here to help his brother run his house painting company, The Paint Saints."

"Oh no," Zibby said quickly. "I don't think my parents need to repaint right now."

Zibby began to intently study the Cheetos so that Mrs. Long couldn't see the look of shock on her face. Because she was finally starting to understand what was going on – Gertrude had lied! About her painting. About the food she ate. And about what her dad did for a living. *And maybe,* Zibby thought, *she'd even lied about* more *things!*

Zibby looked up. "Gertrude is such an interesting name," she said. "Was she named after anyone special?"

"Yes," smiled Mrs. Long. "My great-aunt. She was quite a character – she spent all her time crocheting hats for her long-haired dachshunds – she had five. We all loved her."

What about Gertrude Stein, the famous author? Zibby wondered. *This was getting weirder and weirder.* She then asked, "Does Gertrude have a sinus problem that means she can't be around vents?" she asked.

"Not that I know of," said Mrs. Long, looking alarmed. "Why, has she been sniffling at school or something?"

"Oh no, she's fine," said Zibby, finishing up the Cheetos and feeling a little sick.

Zibby began to nervously push the bowl around the table when the cover of a book caught her attention. Something about the painting on the cover – by an artist named Jackson Pollock – seemed familiar to her.

She wiped her orange fingers on her jeans and began to flip through the pages. And there, on page 133, she saw something that took her breath away. It was Gertrude's painting. The same shapes-floating-in-an-ocean-or-sky. Her *award-winning* painting ... which turns out really wasn't her painting at all!

"Are you a fan of Jackson Pollock?" asked Mrs. Long. "He's one of Gertrude's favorite artists."

"I've seen his work before, but I never knew who the artist was," she said, closing the book and feeling as if she'd better get going. But before she did, she couldn't resist asking two more questions.

"Mrs. Long, what do you do?"

"I'm a freelance writer – I write grants for a non-profit organization. My, you certainly are inquisitive – not that it's bad or anything."

"I know," Zibby said apologetically. "I always ask a lot of questions. But if you don't mind, can I ask just one more?"

"Sure, honey," said Mrs. Long.

"Does Gertrude have two brothers?"

"Yes – Jules is a sophomore in high school and Robert's in fourth grade. Now, is there anything else you'd like to know?" She smiled kindly.

"I think I've asked enough questions today," said Zibby, feeling better to learn that at least *everything* Gertrude hadn't told her was a lie. "And I'd better get going – thanks again," she said.

"You're welcome, and it was really nice to meet you, Zibby," said Mrs. Long.

"You, too," said Zibby, even though considering what she'd learned from Mrs. Long, she couldn't be 100 percent sincere!

"Now what am I going to do?" she asked herself as she left the Long house and headed off to the knitting store. Should she tell Gertrude she'd learned the truth, or would it be mean to put Gertrude on the spot? But if she didn't tell Gertrude, how could she be around her ever again knowing that half the things she said about herself were untrue?

And what about Sarah? Should Zibby be the one to tell her? Or would it be better if she learned about it from Gertrude?

Ugh, she sighed. Just when she though this Friendship Fiasco couldn't get any worse ... it did! A whole lot worse!

CHAPTER 15

THE STORIES UNRAVEL

When Zibby arrived at the knitting store, she found Sarah sitting outside alone.

"Hey, what are you doing here?" asked Sarah, greeting her with a smile and jumping up to give her a little hug.

"I decided that if I ever wanted to see you two, I'd have to start knitting," Zibby said as she hugged Sarah back.

"Really?" asked Sarah. "That's awesome – as long as you can stand it though."

"I'm going to try," said Zibby. "I went over to Gertrude's house to find you, since you two weren't answering your phones, and her mom said you were here."

"Oh yeah – we had to turn them off because the lady in this store won't help you if your cell phone rings," said Sarah, pulling her phone out of her purse and turning it back on.

"So where's Gertrude?" asked Zibby.

"She ran back inside to ask about this stitch we want to try," said Sarah.

Zibby still wasn't sure what she was going to say or do, and she was trying her best to act normal, but the next thing she knew, she blurted out: "Have you ever been over to

Gertrude's house or have you met her family?"

"No, not yet," said Sarah, looking at Zibby quizzically. "Why do you ask?"

"Because when I was at her house today I talked a lot to her mom and I learned some pretty weird stuff."

"Like what?" asked Sarah.

"It turns out that there isn't any award-winning painting in the living room like Gertrude said!" Zibby continued.

"So, maybe her parents moved it," said Sarah.

"No! There isn't one. At all. That award-winning painting isn't hers. It's in a book about a famous painter named Jackson P-something. It's *his* painting, not hers."

Sarah looked at her as if she was crazy. "What are you talking about, Zibby?"

"And," Zibby kept on going, "I learned that her dad isn't an artist – he paints houses – and she doesn't have sinus problems and she wasn't named after a famous writer. She was named after this great-aunt who made dog hats!"

"What?" asked Sarah, frowning.

"And she eats junk food! Listen to this – her mom gave me *Cheetos* to eat! Look" – she threw open her hands and showed Sarah her orange-stained fingers. "I'm telling you, Sarah, Gertrude made up half the stuff she told us about herself."

"Why would she do that?" asked Sarah.

"I don't know," said Zibby. "But she did!"

Sarah looked at her curiously for a moment, then she got a knowing look on her face.

"Oh, Zibby. You don't have to do this."

"Do what?"

"I know what's happening. I've been there – when you and Gertrude were first friends. I know how bad it can feel. But don't do this."

"But I'm not doing anything!" yelled Zibby.

"I get it. Gertrude and I have been so wrapped up in knitting, we've totally been ignoring you. You're feeling left out so you're making up all these stories about Gertrude. To turn me against her. But you're still my best friend, Zibby, even if I am friends with Gertrude."

"I'm not making up anything," said Zibby. "I do hate knitting and maybe I have been feeling left out, but that's not what this is about!"

"I won't tell Gertrude what you said," Sarah continued, "but I will tell her we should quit knitting and instead do something you want to do this weekend."

Zibby sighed. While she was happy she was finally going to get to spend time with Sarah and Gertrude, how could she enjoy it after what she'd discovered?

Just then Gertrude came out of the shop carrying a small sack. "Hi, Zibby." She looked surprised to see her. "What's up?"

"I came to knit with you," Zibby said, suddenly feeling so awkward she could hardly stand to be around Gertrude. She'd have to tell Gertrude she knew the truth. Otherwise, the lies would just sit between her and Gertrude like the Great Wall of China.

"Hey, is something wrong?" asked Gertrude, sensing Zibby's nervousness.

Before Zibby could answer, Sarah quickly said, "Zibby's feeling as if she'd like to hang out with us, but she doesn't want to knit, so I think to include her, we should do something else."

"Oh, well, sure," said Gertrude. "We could always – "

"Actually something *is* wrong, but that's not it," Zibby interrupted. "Well, that is it, too, but there's something more important we've got to talk about. I went to your house today and I met your mom."

"You went to my house?" asked Gertrude, stiffening.

"Yes, and we got to talking, and a few things came up – things that don't make a lot of sense," Zibby continued.

"Oh really?" asked Gertrude, her voice dropping.

"Yes, like about your painting and how you got your name and what your dad does," said Zibby.

"Why'd you go over there anyway?" Gertrude lashed out. "I never invited you."

"I was looking for you and Sarah," said Zibby.

Gertrude bit her lip and then she sat down with a big sigh on a bench in front of the shop.

"Are you okay?" asked Zibby.

"I'm fine," she said.

"So, I don't understand," said Zibby, "why you made all that stuff up."

"What stuff?" said Sarah, who had been watching the exchange between Zibby and Gertrude with growing confusion. "So" – she turned to Gertrude – "what Zibby's been saying about your painting and your dad and your name is true?"

"Yes," Gertrude said sharply, looking up at Sarah. "I lied about some things. There! Are you happy?"

Sarah's face fell. "No," she said in a quiet voice.

"But why did you do it?" persisted Zibby. "I don't get it."

"I swear, I didn't mean to, but the lies just sort of fell out of my mouth," answered Gertrude. "Then once they did, others came out, and then I had to pretend like it was all true. I tried to tell you once, but I got interrupted, and then I just never did."

"But I don't get why you lied in the first place," said Zibby.

"This is the third time we've moved in a year and a half. I know I talk a lot about how great things were in Oakville, but actually I only lived there a few months and I hardly had any friends. My dad has changed jobs a lot recently, and now he's moved here to work with my uncle, and I had to start all over – again!

"I hate being the new girl. So on that first day at school, to impress Amber, I made up the stuff about my dad being an artist and about the award-winning painting. Then I made up the other stuff to impress you too, like about my name. Because it's bad enough being new without having such a dorky name."

"Hey, I love your name," protested Zibby. But Gertrude

just rolled her eyes.

"What about the health food, then," said Zibby. "Why'd you make that up?"

"Oh, it was so stupid," cried out Gertrude. "I was just trying to show you I was cool and not like everyone else. I even started eating veggie chips because of it. And I don't even like them!"

"Wow, I thought they were kinda tasty," said Zibby, remembering they weren't half-bad. Then she had another thought: "So that explains why you ate ice cream with me but not with Sarah."

Gertrude nodded, looking as if she might cry.

"And the vent – Zibby said you don't *really* have sinus problems," said Sarah.

"I feel really bad about that one," said Gertrude. "I didn't know you then, or I never would have picked your desk. I was just trying to be different, again – and point out something about the vent that maybe no one thought of before.

"I know you think it's terrible. But *you* try moving to a bunch of new places and fitting in!"

Zibby actually didn't think what Gertrude had done was terrible, even though she was surprised by her revelations. She really couldn't blame Gertrude for her fibs, considering she herself had lied herself to Gertrude and Sarah during Operation Friendship – even if they were small fibs and were meant to serve a good purpose. Plus, there was one time in her life she'd told a big lie, and a mean one to boot, so you could even say she was worse than Gertrude.

"Just so you know," said Gertrude, "I really do have two brothers and my mom does drive a Prius."

"I know – I saw it," said Zibby.

"And I was a tomboy in second grade." She looked at Zibby.

"I believe you," said Zibby.

"Well, I'm glad you believe me about something because I'm sure after this, you'll never trust me again." Gertrude stood up and wiped her eyes with her sweater sleeve. "I gotta go," she said, then she began walking quickly down the street.

"Hey, wait a minute," Zibby called out to her, but Gertrude just ignored her, and then broke into a run.

CHAPTER 16

MUSIC TO THEIR EARS

"I still can't believe it," said Sarah. The two girls had gone over to Zibby's house after the Knitting Store Scene and were sitting in Zibby's room talking about what had happened.

"The weird thing is, she didn't need to lie at all. She's already cool and different enough!" said Zibby.

"And I would have liked her better if she hadn't stolen my desk and if she'd liked the Cabinet of Carbs," said Sarah. "Plus, who cares what her dad does or if she's won any awards or who she was named after?"

"Yeah, but Amber did put her on the spot, and you know how Amber can be," said Zibby.

"Maybe my first impression of her was right," Sarah shook her head. "I knew something was wrong. I didn't like her and now it turns out there was a reason."

"Sarah!" said Zibby sharply. "If you're saying you don't like her anymore just because she stretched the truth to fit in, after all I've done to get you to be friends – including spending this whole last week on my own – well, I'm just going to throw myself down as a sacrifice to the Friendship Gods!"

"I never said I didn't like her anymore – I just said I

knew something was off and I *used* to not like her," protested Sarah. "But that was before I got to know her. I do still want to be her friend. She's talented and nice and interesting, and those things aren't lies." She paused for a moment. "And by the way, I'm sorry we ignored you this week."

"It's okay," said Zibby. And it was. She knew Sarah hadn't meant to leave her out. Just like she hadn't meant to leave Sarah out. She was already past *that*. She was thinking of what to do *now*.

"Hey, maybe we should go over to her house and tell her we still want to be her friend," Zibby yelled, jumping up. "We could be there in like ten minutes."

"I think maybe she needs some space right now – it might be too overwhelming for her," said Sarah.

"That's a good point," Zibby agreed.

But still, they had to do something. Something to reassure Gertrude. And something to once and for all patch up this vexing friendship between the three girls that always seemed to leave one of them out.

Then suddenly Zibby was hit with another one of her Very Good Ideas. She'd heard Anthony talking about an electronic device that just might do the trick to getting the three girls on track. Maybe it wouldn't fix things forever. Or make Gertrude feel as if she never had to lie again. Or guarantee they'd all stay friends.

But it felt right. And she thought it would feel right to Sarah too.

She quickly filled Sarah in on her plan, and Sarah

agreed. They arranged to meet on the blacktop Monday morning, where once and for all, Zibby was hoping, they could finally put all this trio trouble behind them.

* * *

However, that Monday morning, Gertrude was nowhere to be seen. She didn't show up on the blacktop. And she wasn't in class either.

"Where *is* she?" asked Zibby impatiently, looking around the classroom just like she'd done on Gertrude's first day of school. She was beginning to lose hope that Gertrude was ever coming when she walked in just as Miss Cannon was starting the math lesson.

Gertrude rushed to her seat and stared straight ahead at the blackboard. Zibby tried to catch her eye and give her a smile, but Gertrude wouldn't look at her.

At recess, Gertrude bolted out of the classroom before Zibby could even try to talk to her. Zibby – with Sarah in tow – followed her to a lunch table where she'd sat down and was pulling out a sketchbook.

The two girls sat down next to her and Zibby asked, "So where were you this morning?"

Gertrude shrugged. "I didn't really want to come to school today, if you must know," she said. "But my mom made me."

"Listen, don't worry – don't worry about anything," said Zibby, pulling out her iPod and some other equipment from her backpack. "Hey, remember how I promised you we'd listen to *Across the Universe*? This thing" – she pointed to a cable – "is called a headphone splitter. It lets you plug two sets of earphones into your iPod, which," she dangled an extra pair of earphones in front of Gertrude's face, "I just happen to have. So now, all three of us can listen to the same song on one iPod – with one earbud to spare! Cool, huh?"

"I guess so," said Gertrude hesitantly.

"So I was thinking, we could all listen to *Across the Universe* together. What do you think? You want to hear it … with us?"

Gertrude just looked at her and then at Sarah.

"Come on, it's a really awesome CD," prodded Zibby.

"Yeah, come on," echoed Sarah.

"Um … oh, sure," said Gertrude, slowly breaking into a smile. "Sounds rad."

Zibby attached the devices to her iPod, then handed each girl an earbud before putting her own in. She turned on the music, and began to bop her head along with the beat. So did Sarah. And then Gertrude.

Maybe three isn't such an odd number after all, Zibby thought to herself, feeling relaxed and happy for the first time in weeks.

But the feeling didn't last long. Because the next thing she knew, Amber was standing in front of them, wearing a neon jacket with huge shoulder pads.

"Don't you just *adore* my *pre-loved* 80s outfit?" Amber asked. "It just came in the mail and my mom dropped it off.

I luv pre-loved – got to show the rest of my peeps," she exclaimed and went running off, shoulder pads sticking out as if she was a linebacker on a professional football team. "Oh, and guess what?" Amber then turned around and added, "I luv this look so much, I'm going to see if we can all wear it for sixth-grade graduation. Later!"

"What?" asked Zibby, looking frantically at Gertrude and then at Sarah. "*I'm* going to have to wear something like *that*?"

The three girls looked at each in horror. Then they began to smile. And then they began to giggle.

All three of them.

Together.

THE END

Looking for more Zibby?
Check out the rest of the series:

Zibby Payne
& the Party Problem
ISBN: 978-1-897073-69-8

When Zibby's "sometimes friends" Amber and Savannah start handing out special party privileges to a select few, Zibby decides to have her own Totally Fair and Equal Party, with an open invitation policy. Find out what happens when her over-the-top party plans get way out of hand – it's one one prickly party predicament!

Zibby Payne
& the Drama Trauma
ISBN: 978-1-897073-47-6

Watch out Broadway, Total Tomboy Zibby has landed the lead in the sixth-grade musical. But if she doesn't stick to the script, it could be curtains for her acting career!

"... readers won't be able to put it down and parents everywhere will approve."
– *Mom Central Book Reviews*

"Zibby Payne's adventures have the humour and momentum to become a well-loved series." – *Montreal Review of Books*

Zibby Payne & the Wonderful, Terrible Tomboy Experiment
ISBN: 978-1-897073-39-1

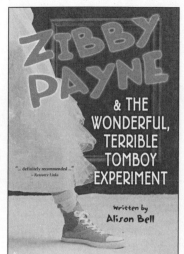

While the girls in her class obsess over lip gloss and boy bands, Zibby goes to extremes to express her True Tomboy self.

"... an outstanding character who sticks to her guns ... readers will learn ... you don't have to change for others to like you, and you should be proud of who you are."
– Bildungsroman Book Blog

"Bell has created a girl who's not afraid to be herself. A rare treat."
– Mary Hogan, author of **The Serious Kiss**

About the author: Alison Bell got her start as an editor at *'TEEN* magazine. She's written for *YM*, *Sassy*, and the *Los Angeles Times*, and is also the author of **Let's Party!** and **Fearless Fashion** from the "What's Your Style?" series (see the next page for info!). Alison lives just outside of Los Angeles in South Pasadena, California.

Visit her online at alisonbellauthor.com

Also from Alison Bell –
the "What's Your Style?" Series

Let's Party
ISBN: 978-1-894222-99-0

Need ideas for your next big bash? **Let's Party!** provides eight cool and complete party plans, like the "Sensational Spa" and the "Spy Thriller Party." With mix n' match party concepts, quizzes, and troubleshooting tips, this is the essential guide for every hostess with the mostest.

"Suggestions are included for food (with recipes), small favors, and 'the setting,' but the emphasis is on the activities ... preparing for the party looks at least as fun as the event itself ..." – *The InGram*

"The ideas are fresh and simple enough for the hostess to accomplish on her own ... This manual is sure to fly off shelves." – *School Library Journal*

Fearless Fashion
ISBN: 978-1-894222-86-0

Ever wonder where different styles come from, and which one suits you best? While deconstructing today's hottest looks, **Fearless Fashion** gives you tidbits of fashion history, shows you trendy celebs and the styles they embrace, and offers creative ways to personalize any look. Includes fun quizzes to take with your friends!

"Girls will enjoy thumbing through this book as their first step into the world of fashion." – *School Library Journal*

"... ideas to adapt looks from 'preppy' to 'punk,' to make them uniquely one's own." – *Publishers Weekly*